Samuel French Acting E

M000317885

The Death of the Last Black Man in the Whole Entire World

AKA The Negro Book of the Dead

by Suzan-Lori Parks

SAMUELFRENCH.COM   SAMUELFRENCH.CO.UK

FOR PRODUCTION ENQUIRIES

UNITED STATES AND CANADA
Info@SamuelFrench.com
1-866-598-8449

UNITED KINGDOM AND EUROPE
Plays@SamuelFrench.co.uk
020-7255-4302

Each title is subject to availability from Samuel French, depending upon country of performance. Please be aware that *THE DEATH OF THE LAST BLACK MAN IN THE WHOLE ENTIRE WORLD* may not be licensed by Samuel French in your territory. Professional and amateur producers should contact the nearest Samuel French office or licensing partner to verify availability.

MUSIC USE NOTE

Licensees are solely responsible for obtaining formal written permission from copyright owners to use copyrighted music in the performance of this play and are strongly cautioned to do so. If no such permission is obtained by the licensee, then the licensee must use only original music that the licensee owns and controls. Licensees are solely responsible and liable for all music clearances and shall indemnify the copyright owners of the play(s) and their licensing agent, Samuel French, against any costs, expenses, losses and liabilities arising from the use of music by licensees. Please contact the appropriate music licensing authority in your territory for the rights to any incidental music.

IMPORTANT BILLING AND CREDIT REQUIREMENTS

If you have obtained performance rights to this title, please refer to your licensing agreement for important billing and credit requirements.

THE DEATH OF THE LAST BLACK MAN IN THE WHOLE ENTIRE WORLD premiered at Signature Theatre's Alice Griffin Jewel Box Theatre in New York City on October 25, 2016. The production was directed by Lileana Blain-Cruz, with scenic design by Riccardo Hernandez, costume design by Montana Blanco, lighting design by Yi Zhao, and sound design by Palmer Hefferan. The production stage manager was Terri K. Kohler. The cast was as follows:

BLACK MAN WITH WATERMELON	Daniel J. Watts
BLACK WOMAN WITH FRIED DRUMSTICK	Roslyn Ruff
LOTS OF GREASE AND LOTS OF PORK	Jamar Williams
YES AND GREENS BLACK-EYED PEAS CORNBREAD	Nike Kadri
QUEEN-THEN-PHARAOH HATSHEPSUT	Amelia Workman
BEFORE COLUMBUS	David Ryan Smith
OLD MAN RIVER JORDAN	Julian Rozzell
HAM	Patrena Murray
AND BIGGER AND BIGGER AND BIGGER	Reynaldo Piniella
PRUNES AND PRISMS	Mirirai Sithole
VOICE ON THUH TEE V	William DeMeritt

CHARACTERS

BLACK MAN WITH WATERMELON
BLACK WOMAN WITH FRIED DRUMSTICK
LOTS OF GREASE AND LOTS OF PORK
YES AND GREENS BLACK-EYED PEAS CORNBREAD
QUEEN-THEN-PHARAOH HATSHEPSUT
BEFORE COLUMBUS
OLD MAN RIVER JORDAN
HAM
AND BIGGER AND BIGGER AND BIGGER
PRUNES AND PRISMS
VOICE ON THUH TEE V

TIME

The Present

When I die,
I won't stay
Dead.

– Bob Kaufman

OVERTURE

BLACK MAN WITH WATERMELON.

The black man moves his hands.

(A bell sounds twice.)

LOTS OF GREASE AND LOTS OF PORK.

Lots of Grease and Lots of Pork.

QUEEN-THEN-PHARAOH HATSHEPSUT.

Queen-then-Pharaoh Hatshepsut.

AND BIGGER AND BIGGER AND BIGGER.

And Bigger and Bigger and Bigger.

PRUNES AND PRISMS.

Prunes and Prisms.

HAM.

Ham.

VOICE ON THUH TEE V.

Voice on Thuh Tee V.

OLD MAN RIVER JORDAN.

Old Man River Jordan.

YES AND GREENS BLACK-EYED PEAS CORNBREAD.

Yes and Greens Black-Eyed Peas Cornbread.

BEFORE COLUMBUS.

Before Columbus.

(A bell sounds once.)

BLACK MAN WITH WATERMELON.

The black man moves his hands.

ALL.

Not yet.

QUEEN-THEN-PHARAOH HATSHEPSUT.

Let Queen-then-Pharaoh Hatshepsut tell you when.

LOTS OF GREASE AND LOTS OF PORK.

This is the death of the last black man in the whole entire world.

(A bell sounds three times.)

BLACK WOMAN WITH FRIED DRUMSTICK.

Yesterday today next summer tomorrow just uh moment uhgoh in 1317 dieded thuh last black man in thuh whole entire world. Uh! Oh. Dont be uhlarmed. Do not be afeared. It was painless. Uh painless passin. He falls twenty-three floors to his death. 23 floors from uh passin ship from space tuh splat on thuh pavement. He have uh head he been keepin under thuh Tee V. On his bottom pantry shelf. He have uh head that hurts. Dont fit right. Put it on tuh go tuh thuh store in it pinched him when he walks his thoughts dont got room. Why dieded he huh? Where he gonna go now that he done dieded? Where he gonna go tuh wash his hands?

YES AND GREENS BLACK-EYED PEAS CORNBREAD.

You should write that down and you should hide it under a rock.

BIGGER AND BIGGER AND BIGGER.

This is the death of the last black man in the whole entire world.

FEMALE CHARACTERS.

Not yet—

BLACK MAN WITH WATERMELON.

The black man moves. His hands—

QUEEN-THEN-PHARAOH HATSHEPSUT.

You are too young to move. Let me move it for you.

BLACK MAN WITH WATERMELON.

The black man moves his hands. —He moves his hands round. Back. Back. Back tuh that.

LOTS OF GREASE AND LOTS OF PORK.

(Not dat.)

BLACK MAN WITH WATERMELON.

When thuh worl usta be roun. Thuh worl usta be *roun*.

BLACK WOMAN WITH FRIED DRUMSTICK.

Uh roun worl. Uh roun? Thuh worl? When was this.

QUEEN-THEN-PHARAOH HATSHEPSUT.

Columbus. Before.

BEFORE COLUMBUS.

Before. Columbus.

YES AND GREENS BLACK-EYED PEAS CORNBREAD.

Before Columbus.

BLACK MAN WITH WATERMELON.

HHH. HA!

QUEEN-THEN-PHARAOH HATSHEPSUT.

Before Columbus thuh worl usta be roun they put uh /d/ on thuh end of roun makin roun*d*. Thusly they set in motion thuh end. Without that /d/ we coulda gone on spinnin forever. Thuh /d/ thing ended things ended.

YES AND GREENS BLACK-EYED PEAS CORNBREAD.

Before Columbus.

(A bell sounds twice.)

BEFORE COLUMBUS.

The popular thinking of the day back in them days was that the world was flat. They thought the world was flat. Back then when they thought the world was flat they were afeared and stayed at home. They wanted to go out back then when they thought the world was flat but the water had in it dragons of which meaning these dragons they were afeared back then when they thought the world was flat. They stayed at home. Them thinking the world was flat kept it roun. Them thinking the sun revolved around the earth kept them satellite-like. They figured out the truth and scurried out. Figuring out the truth put them in their place and they scurried out to put us in ours.

YES AND GREENS BLACK-EYED PEAS CORNBREAD.

Mmmm. Yes. You should write this down. You should hide this under a rock.

LOTS OF GREASE AND LOTS OF PORK & PRUNES AND PRISMS.

Not yet—

BLACK MAN WITH WATERMELON.

The black man bursts into flames. The black man bursts into blames. Whose fault is it?

ALL.

Aint mines.

BLACK MAN WITH WATERMELON.

Whose fault is it?

ALL.

Aint mines.

BLACK WOMAN WITH FRIED DRUMSTICK.

I cant remember back that far.

QUEEN-THEN-PHARAOH HATSHEPSUT.

And besides, I wasnt even there.

BLACK MAN WITH WATERMELON.

Ha ha ha. The black man laughs out loud.

ALL. *(Except* **HAM.***)*

HAM-BONE-HAM-BONE-WHERE-YOU-BEEN-ROUN-THUH-WORL-N-BACK-UH-GAIN.

YES AND GREENS BLACK-EYED PEAS CORNBREAD.

Whatcha seen hambone girl?

BLACK WOMAN WITH FRIED DRUMSTICK.

Didnt see you. I saw thuh worl.

QUEEN-THEN-PHARAOH HATSHEPSUT.

I was there.

LOTS OF GREASE AND LOTS OF PORK.

Didnt see you.

BIGGER AND BIGGER AND BIGGER.

I was there.

VOICE ON THUH TEE V.

Didnt see you.

HAM.

I was there.

OLD MAN RIVER JORDAN.

Didnt see you.

BLACK WOMAN WITH FRIED DRUMSTICK.

I was there.

PRUNES AND PRISMS.

Didnt see you.

BLACK MAN WITH WATERMELON.

The black man moves his hands.

QUEEN-THEN-PHARAOH HATSHEPSUT.

We are too young to see. Let them see it for you. We are too young to rule. Let them rule it for you. We are too young to have. Let them have it for you. You are too young to write. Let them—let them. Do it. Before you.

BLACK MAN WITH WATERMELON.

The black man moves his hands.

YES AND GREENS BLACK-EYED PEAS CORNBREAD.

You should write it down because if you dont write it down then they will come along and tell the future that we did not exist. You should write it down and you should hide it under a rock. You should write down the past and you should write down the present and in what in the future you should write it down.

PRUNES AND PRISMS.

It will be of us but you should mention them from time to time

YES AND GREENS BLACK EYED PEAS CORNBREAD.

so that in the future when they come along and know that they exist.

PRUNES AND PRISMS.

You should hide it all under a rock

YES AND GREENS BLACK EYED PEAS CORNBREAD.

so that in the future when they come along they will say that the rock did not exist.

BLACK WOMAN WITH FRIED DRUMSTICK.

We getting somewheres. We getting down. Down down down down down down down down—

QUEEN-THEN-PHARAOH HATSHEPSUT.

I saw Columbus comin. / I saw Columbus comin goin over tuh visit you. "To borrow a cup of sugar," so he said. I waved my hands in warnin. You waved back. I aint seen you since.

LOTS OF GREASE AND LOTS OF PORK.

In the future when they came along I meeting them. On thuh coast.

LOTS OF GREASE AND LOTS OF PORK & BIGGER AND BIGGER AND BIGGER.

Uh! Thuh Coast!

HAM.

I—was—so—polite.

LOTS OF GREASE AND LOTS OF PORK & VOICE ON THUH TEE V.

But in thuh dirt, I wrote:

OLD MAN RIVER JORDAN.

"Ha. Ha. Ha."

ALL.

Ha. Ha. Ha. Ha. Ha. Ha. Ha. Ha. Ha. Ha. Ha. Ha. Ha. Ha. Ha. Ha. HHHHHHHHHHHHHHHH.

BLACK MAN WITH WATERMELON.

Thuh black man he move. He move he hans.

(A bell sounds once.)

PANEL I: THUH HOLY GHOST

BLACK MAN WITH WATERMELON.

Saint mines. Saint mines. Iduhnt it. Nope: iduhnt. Saint mines cause everythin I calls mines got uh print uh me someway on it in it dont got uh print uh me someway on it so saint mines. Duhduhnt so saint: huh.

BLACK WOMAN WITH FRIED DRUMSTICK.

Hen.

BLACK MAN WITH WATERMELON.

Huh. Huh?

BLACK WOMAN WITH FRIED DRUMSTICK.

Hen. Hen?

BLACK MAN WITH WATERMELON.

Who give birth tuh this I wonder. Who gived birth tuh this. I wonder.

BLACK WOMAN WITH FRIED DRUMSTICK.

You comed back. Comin backs somethin in itself. You comed back.

BLACK MAN WITH WATERMELON.

This does not belong tuh me. Somebody planted this on me. On me in my hands.

BLACK WOMAN WITH FRIED DRUMSTICK.

Cold compress. Cold compress then some hen. Lean back. You comed back. Lean back.

BLACK MAN WITH WATERMELON.

Who gived birth tuh this I wonder who.

BLACK WOMAN WITH FRIED DRUMSTICK.

Comin for you. Came for you: that they done did. Comin for tuh take you. Told me tuh pack up your clothes. Told me tuh cut my bed in 2 from double tuh single. Cut off thuh bed-foot where your feets had rested. Told me tuh do that too. Burry your ring in his hidin spot under thuh porch! That they told me too to do. Didnt have uh ring so I didnt do diddly. They told and told and told: proper instructions for thuh burial proper attire for thuh mournin. They told and told and told: I didnt do squat. Awe on that. You comed back. You got uhway. Knew you would. Hen?

BLACK MAN WITH WATERMELON.

Who gived birth tuh this I wonder. Who? Not me. Saint mines.

BLACK WOMAN WITH FRIED DRUMSTICK.

Killed every hen on thuh block. You comed back. Knew you would. Knew you would came back. Knew you will wanted uh good big hen dinner in waitin. Every hen on the block.

BLACK MAN WITH WATERMELON.

Saint mines.

BLACK WOMAN WITH FRIED DRUMSTICK.

Strutted down on up thuh road with my axe. By-my-self-with-my-axe. Got tuh thuh street top 93 dyin hen din hand. Dropped thuh axe. Tooked tuh stranglin. 93 dyin hen din hand with no heads let em loose tuh run down tuh towards home infront of me. Flipped thuh necks of thuh next 23 more odd. Slinged um over my shoulders. Hens of thuh neighbors now in my pots. Feathers of thuh hens of thuh neighbors stucked in our mattress. They told and told and told. On me. Huh. Awe on that. Hen? You got uhway. Knew you would.

BLACK MAN WITH WATERMELON.

Who gived birth tuh me I wonder.

BLACK WOMAN WITH FRIED DRUMSTICK.

They dont speak tuh us no more. They pass by our porch but they dont nod. You been comed back goin on 9 years not even heard from thuh neighbors uh congratulation. Uh alienationed dum. Uh guess. Huh. Hen? *WE AINT GOT NO FRIENDS*, —sweetheart.

BLACK MAN WITH WATERMELON.

SWEET-HEART.

BLACK WOMAN WITH FRIED DRUMSTICK.

Hen!!

BLACK MAN WITH WATERMELON.

Aint hungry.

BLACK WOMAN WITH FRIED DRUMSTICK.

Hen.

BLACK MAN WITH WATERMELON.

Aint eaten in years.

BLACK WOMAN WITH FRIED DRUMSTICK.

Hen?

BLACK MAN WITH WATERMELON.

Last meal I had was my last-mans-meal.

BLACK WOMAN WITH FRIED DRUMSTICK.

You got uhway. Knew you would.

BLACK MAN WITH WATERMELON.

This thing dont look like me!

BLACK WOMAN WITH FRIED DRUMSTICK.

It dont. Do it. Should it? Hen: eat it.

BLACK MAN WITH WATERMELON.

I kin tell whats mines by whats gots my looks. Ssmymethod. Try it by testin it and it turns out true. Every time. Fool proofly. Look down at my foot and wonder if its mine. Foot mine? I kin ask it and foot answers back with uh "yes Sir"—not like you and me say "yes Sir" but uh "yes Sir" peculiar tuh thuh foot. Foot mine? I kin ask it and through uh look that looks like my looks thuh foot gives me back uh "yes Sir." Ssmymethod. Try by thuh test tuh pass for true. Move on tuh thuh uther foot. Foot mine? And uh nother "yes Sir" so feets mine is understood. Got uh forearm thats up for question check myself out teeth by tooth. Melon mines? —. Dont look like me.

BLACK WOMAN WITH FRIED DRUMSTICK.

Hen mine? Gobble it up and it will be. You got uhway. Fixed uh good big hen dinner for you. Get yourself uh mouthful afore it rots.

BLACK MAN WITH WATERMELON.

Was we green and stripedly when we first comed out?

BLACK WOMAN WITH FRIED DRUMSTICK.

Uh huhn. Thuh features comes later. Later comes after now.

BLACK MAN WITH WATERMELON.

Oh. Later comes now: melon mine?

BLACK WOMAN WITH FRIED DRUMSTICK.

They comed from you and tooked you. That was yesterday. Today you sit in your chair where you sat yesterday and thuh day afore yesterday afore they comed and tooked you. Things today is just as they are yesterday cept nothin is familiar cause it was such uh long time uhgoh.

BLACK MAN WITH WATERMELON.

Later oughta be now by now huh?: melon mine?

BLACK WOMAN WITH FRIED DRUMSTICK.

Thuh chair was portable. They take it from county tuh county. Only got one. Can only eliminate one at uh time. Woulda fried you right here on thuh front porch but we dont got enough electric. No onessgot enough electric. Not on our block. Dont believe in havin enough. Put thuh Chair in thuh middle of thuh City. Outdoors. In thuh square. Folks come tuh watch with picnic baskets. —Hen?

BLACK MAN WITH WATERMELON.

Sweetheart?

BLACK WOMAN WITH FRIED DRUMSTICK.

They juiced you some, huh?

BLACK MAN WITH WATERMELON.

Just a squirt. Sweetheart.

BLACK WOMAN WITH FRIED DRUMSTICK.
Humpty Dumpty.

BLACK MAN WITH WATERMELON.
Melon mines?

BLACK WOMAN WITH FRIED DRUMSTICK.
Humpty damn Dumpty actin like thuh Holy Ghost.
You got uhway. Thuh lights dimmed but you got uhway.
Knew you would.

BLACK MAN WITH WATERMELON.
They juiced me some.

BLACK WOMAN WITH FRIED DRUMSTICK.
Just a squirt.

BLACK MAN WITH WATERMELON.
They had theirselves uh extender chord. Fry uh man in
thuh town square needs uh extender tuh reach em thuh
electric. Hook up thuh chair tuh thuh power. Extender:
49 foot in length. Closer tuh thuh power I never been.
Flip on up thuh go switch. Huh! Juice begins its course.

BLACK WOMAN WITH FRIED DRUMSTICK.
Humpty damn Dumpty.

BLACK MAN WITH WATERMELON.
Thuh straps they have on me are leathern. See thuh
cord waggin full with uh jump-juice try me tuh wiggle
from thuh waggin but belt leathern straps: width
thickly. One round each forearm. Forearm mines? 2
cross thuh chest. Chest is mines: and it explodin. One
for my left hand fingers left strapted too. Right was
done thuh same. Jump-juice meets me-mine juices
I do uh slow softshoe like on water. Town crier cries
uh moan. Felt my nappy head go frizzly. Town follows
thuh crier in uh sorta sing-uhlong-song.

BLACK WOMAN WITH FRIED DRUMSTICK.
Then you got uhway. Got uhway in comed back.

BLACK MAN WITH WATERMELON.
Uh extender chord 49 foot in length. Turned on thuh
up switch in I started runnin. First 49 foot I was runnin
they was still juicin.

BLACK WOMAN WITH FRIED DRUMSTICK.

And they chaseted you.

BLACK MAN WITH WATERMELON.

—Melon mines?

BLACK WOMAN WITH FRIED DRUMSTICK.

When you broked tuh seek your freedom they followed after, huh?

BLACK MAN WITH WATERMELON.

Later oughta be now by now, huh?

BLACK WOMAN WITH FRIED DRUMSTICK.

You comed back.

BLACK MAN WITH WATERMELON.

—Not exactly.

BLACK WOMAN WITH FRIED DRUMSTICK.

They comed for you tuh take you. Tooked you uhway: that they done did. You got uhway. Thuh lights dimmed. Had us uh brownout. You got past that. You comed back.

BLACK MAN WITH WATERMELON.

Turned on thuh juice on me in me in I started runnin. First just runnin then runnin towards home. Couldnt find us. Think I got lost. Saw us on up uhhead but I flew over thuh yard. Couldnt stop. Think I overshot.

BLACK WOMAN WITH FRIED DRUMSTICK.

Killed every hen on thuh block. Made you uh—

BLACK MAN WITH WATERMELON.

Make me uh space 6 feet by 6 feet by 6. Make it big and mark it so as I wont miss it. If you would please, sweetness, uh mass grave-site. Theres company comin soonish. I would like tuh get up and go. I would like tuh move my hands.

BLACK WOMAN WITH FRIED DRUMSTICK.

You comed back.

BLACK MAN WITH WATERMELON.

Overshot. Overshot. I would like tuh move my hands.

BLACK WOMAN WITH FRIED DRUMSTICK.
Cold compress?

BLACK MAN WITH WATERMELON.
Sweetheart.

BLACK WOMAN WITH FRIED DRUMSTICK.
How uhbout uh hen leg?

BLACK MAN WITH WATERMELON.
Nothanks. Justate.

BLACK WOMAN WITH FRIED DRUMSTICK.
Just ate?

BLACK MAN WITH WATERMELON.
Thatsright. 6 by 6 by 6. Thatsright

BLACK WOMAN WITH FRIED DRUMSTICK.
Oh. —. They eat their own yuh know.

BLACK MAN WITH WATERMELON.
HooDoo.

BLACK WOMAN WITH FRIED DRUMSTICK.
Hen do. Saw it on thuh Tee V.

BLACK MAN WITH WATERMELON.
Aint that nice.

(A bell sounds once.)

PANEL II: FIRST CHORUS

BLACK MAN WITH WATERMELON.
6 by 6 by 6.

ALL.
THATS RIGHT.

BLACK WOMAN WITH FRIED DRUMSTICK.
Oh. They eat their own you know.

ALL.
HOODOO.

BLACK WOMAN WITH FRIED DRUMSTICK.
Hen do. Saw it on thuh Tee V.

ALL.
Aint that nice.

AND BIGGER AND BIGGER AND BIGGER.
WILL SOMEBODY TAKE THESE STRAPS OFF UH ME PLEASE? I WOULD LIKE TUH MOVE MY HANDS.

PRUNES AND PRISMS.
Prunes and prisms will begin: prunes and prisms prunes and prisms prunes and prisms and prunes and prisms: 23.

VOICE ON THUH TEE V.
Good evening. Im Broad Caster. Headlining tonight: the news: is Gamble Major, the absolutely last living Negro man in the whole entire known world—is dead. Major, Gamble, born a slave, taught himself the rudiments of education to become a spearhead in the Civil Rights Movement. He was 38 years old. News of Majors death sparked controlled displays of jubilation in all corners of the world.

PRUNES AND PRISMS.
Oh no no: world is roun.

AND BIGGER AND BIGGER AND BIGGER.
WILL SOMEBODY TAKE THESE STRAPS OFF UH ME PLEASE? I WOULD LIKE TUH MOVE MY HANDS.

(A bell sounds four times.)

LOTS OF GREASE AND LOTS OF PORK.

This is the death of the last black man in the whole entire world.

PRUNES AND PRISMS.

Not yet—

VOICE ON THUH TEE V.

Good evening. Broad Caster. Headline tonight: Gamble Major, the absolutely last living Negro man in the whole known entire world is dead. Gamble Major born a slave rose to become a spearhead in the Civil Rights Movement. He was 38 years old. The Civil Rights Movement. He was 38 years old.

AND BIGGER AND BIGGER AND BIGGER.

WILL SOMEBODY TAKE THESE STRAPS OFF UH ME PLEASE? I WOULD LIKE TUH MOVE MY HANDS.

LOTS OF GREASE AND LOTS OF PORK.

This is the death of the last black man in the whole entire world.

(A bell sounds three times.)

PRUNES AND PRISMS.

Prunes and prisms prunes and prisms prunes and prisms prunes and prisms.

QUEEN-THEN-PHARAOH HATSHEPSUT.

Yesterday tuhday next summer tuhmorrow just uh moment uhgoh in 1317 dieded thuh last black man in thuh whole entire world. Uh! Oh. Dont be uhlarmed. Do not be afeared. It was painless. Uh painless passin. He falls 23 floors to his death.

BLACK WOMAN WITH FRIED DRUMSTICK.

No.

QUEEN-THEN-PHARAOH HATSHEPSUT.

23 floors from uh passin ship from space tuh splat on thuh pavement.

BLACK WOMAN WITH FRIED DRUMSTICK.

No.

QUEEN-THEN-PHARAOH HATSHEPSUT.

He have uh head he been keepin under thuh Tee V. On his bottom pantry shelf.

BLACK WOMAN WITH FRIED DRUMSTICK.

No.

QUEEN-THEN-PHARAOH HATSHEPSUT.

He have uh head that hurts. Dont fit right. Put it on tuh go tuh thuh store in it pinched him when he walks his thoughts dont got room. Why dieded he huh?

BLACK WOMAN WITH FRIED DRUMSTICK.

No.

QUEEN-THEN-PHARAOH HATSHEPSUT.

Where he gonna go now that he done dieded?

PRUNES AND PRISMS.

No.

BLACK WOMAN WITH FRIED DRUMSTICK.

Where he gonna go tuh wash his hands?

ALL.

You should write that down. You should write that down and you should hide it under uh rock.

VOICE ON THUH TEE V.

Good evening. Broad Caster. Headlinin tonight: thuh news:

OLD MAN RIVER JORDAN.

Tell you of uh news. Last news. Last news of thuh last man. Last man had last words say hearin it. He spoked uh speech spoked hisself uh chatter-tooth babble "ya-oh-may/chuh-naw" dribblin down his lips tuh puddle in his lap. Dribblin by droppletts. Drop by drop. Last news. News flashes then drops. Thuh last drop was uh all uhlone drop. Singular. Thuh last drop started it off it all. Started off with uh drop. Started off with uh jungle. Started sproutin in his spittle growin leaves off of his mines and thuh vines say drippin doin it. Last

news leads tuh thuh first news. He is dead he crosses
thuh river. He jumps in thuh puddle have his clothing:
ON. On thuh other side thuh mountin yo he dripply
wet with soppin. Do drop be dripted? I say "yes."

BLACK MAN WITH WATERMELON.

Dont leave me hear. Dont leave me. Hear?

QUEEN-THEN-PHARAOH HATSHEPSUT.

Where he gonna go tuh wash his dribblin hands?

PRUNES AND PRISMS.

Where he gonna go tuh dry his dripplin clothes?

YES AND GREENS BLACK-EYED PEAS CORNBREAD.

Did you write it down? On uh little slip uh paper stick
thuh slip in thuh river afore you slip in that way you
keep your clothes dry, man.

PRUNES AND PRISMS.

Aintcha heard uh that trick?

BEFORE COLUMBUS.

That tricks thuh method.

QUEEN-THEN-PHARAOH HATSHEPSUT.

They used it on uhlong uhgoh still works every time.

OLD MAN RIVER JORDAN.

He jumped in thuh water without uh word for partin
come out dripply wet with soppin. Do drop be dripted?
I say "do."

BLACK MAN WITH WATERMELON.

In you all theres kin. You all kin. Kin gave thuh first
permission kin be givin it now still. Some things is
all thuh ways gonna be uh continuin sort of uh some
thing. Some things go on and on till they dont stop.
I am soppin wet. I left my scent behind in uh bundle
of old clothing that was not thrown out. Left thuh
scent in thuh clothin in thuh clothin on uh rooftop.
Dogs surround my house and laugh. They are mockin
thuh scent that I left behind. I jumped in thuh water
without uh word. I jumped in thuh water without uh
smell. I am in thuh river and in my skin is soppin wet.

I would like tuh stay afloat now. I would like tuh move
my hands.

AND BIGGER AND BIGGER AND BIGGER.

Would somebody take these straps off uh me please? I
would like tuh move my hands.

BLACK MAN WITH WATERMELON.

Now kin kin I move my hands?

QUEEN-THEN-PHARAOH HATSHEPSUT.

My black man my subject man my man uh all mens
my my my no no not yes no not yes thuh hands. Let
Queen-then-Pharaoh Hatshepsut tell you when. She is
I am. An I am she passing by with her train.

Pulling it behind her on uh plastic chain. Ooooh who!
Oooooh who! Where you gonna go now, now that you
done dieded?

ALL.

Ha ha ha.

PRUNES AND PRISMS.

Say "prunes and prisms" 40 times each day and youll
cure your big lips. Prunes and prisms prunes and
prisms prunes and prisms: 19.

ALL. (*Except* **PRUNES AND PRISMS.**)

Ha ha ha.

QUEEN-THEN-PHARAOH HATSHEPSUT.

An I am Sheba-like she be me am passin on by she with
her train. Pullin it behind/he on uh plastic chain. Oooh
who! Oooh who! Come uhlong. Come uhlong.

BLACK WOMAN WITH FRIED DRUMSTICK.

Say he was waitin on thuh right time.

AND BIGGER AND BIGGER AND BIGGER.

Say he was waitin in thuh wrong line.

BLACK MAN WITH WATERMELON.

I jumped in thuh river without uh word. My kin are
soppin wet.

QUEEN-THEN-PHARAOH HATSHEPSUT.

Come uhlong. Come uhlong.

PRUNES AND PRISMS.

Prunes and prisms prunes and prisms.

LOTS OF GREASE AND LOTS OF PORK.

This is the death of the last black man in the whole entire world.

PRUNES AND PRISMS.

Not yet.

LOTS OF GREASE AND LOTS OF PORK & HAM.

Back tuh when thuh worl usta be roun.

QUEEN-THEN-PHARAOH HATSHEPSUT.

Come uhlong come uhlong get on board come uhlong.

OLD MAN RIVER JORDAN.

Backtuhthat. Yes.

YES AND GREENS BLACK-EYED PEAS CORNBREAD & HAM.

Back tuh when thuh worl usta be roun.

OLD MAN RIVER JORDAN.

Uhcross thuh river in back tuh that. Yes. Do in diddly dip didded thuh drop. Out to thuh river uhlong to thuh sea. Long thuh long coast. Skirtin. Yes. Skirtin back tuh that. Come up back flip take uhway like thuh waves do. Far uhway. Uhway tuh where they dont speak thuh language and where they dont want tuh.

ALL.

Huh.

OLD MAN RIVER JORDAN.

Go on back tuh that.

YES AND GREENS BLACK-EYED PEAS CORNBREAD.

Awe on uh interior before uh demarcation made it mapped. Awe on uh interior with out uh road-word called macadam. Awe onin uh interior that was uh whole was once. Awe on uh whole roun worl uh roun worl with uh river.

HAM.

In thuh interior was uh river.

OLD MAN RIVER JORDAN.

Huh. Back tuh that.

ALL.

Thuh river was roun as thuh worl was. Roun.

OLD MAN RIVER JORDAN.

He hacks his way through thuh tall grass. Tall grass scratch. Width: thickly. Grasses thickly comin from all angles at im. He runs along thuh path worn out by uh 9 million paddin bare footed feet. Uh path overgrown cause it aint as all as happened as of yet. Tuh be extracted from thuh jungle first he gotta go in hide.

BLACK MAN WITH WATERMELON.

Chase-ted me outa thuh trees now they tree me. Thuh dogs come out from their hidin spots under thuh porch and give me uhway. Thuh hidin spot was under thuh porch of uh house that werent there as of yet. Thuh dogs give me uhway by uh laugh aimed at my scent.

AND BIGGER AND BIGGER AND BIGGER.

HA HA HA. Thats how thuh laugh sorta like be wentin.

PRUNES AND PRISMS.

Where he gonna go now now that he done dieded?

QUEEN-THEN-PHARAOH HATSHEPSUT.

Where he gonna go tuh move his hands?

BLACK MAN WITH WATERMELON.

I. I. I would like tuh move my hands.

YES AND GREENS BLACK-EYED PEAS CORNBREAD & HAM.

Back tuh when thuh worl usta be roun.

LOTS OF GREASE AND LOTS OF PORK.

Uh roun. Thuh worl?

LOTS OF GREASE AND LOTS OF PORK & VOICE ON THUH TEE V.

Uh roun worl? When was this?

OLD MAN RIVER JORDAN.

Columbus. Before.

PRUNES AND PRISMS, AND BIGGER AND BIGGER AND BIGGER & VOICE ON THUH TEE V.

Before Columbus?

ALL.

Ho!

QUEEN-THEN-PHARAOH HATSHEPSUT.

Before Columbus thuh worl usta be roun. They put uh /d/ on thuh end of roun makin round. Thusly they set in motion thuh enduh. Without that /d/ we could uh gone on spinnin forever. Thuh /d/ thing endiduh things endiduh.

BEFORE COLUMBUS.

Before Columbus:

(A bell sounds once.)

Thuh popular thinkin kin of thuh day back then in them days was that thuh worl was flat. They thought thuh worl was flat. Back then kin in them days when they thought thuh worl was flat they were afeared and stayed at home. They wanted tuh go out back then when they thought thuh worl was flat but thuh water had in it dragons.

AND BIGGER AND BIGGER AND BIGGER.

Not lurkin in thuh sea but lurkin in thuh street, see? Sir name Tom-us and Bigger be my christian name. Rise up out of uh made-up story in grown Bigger and Bigger. Too big for my own name. Nostrils: flarin. Width: thickly. Breath: fire-laden and smellin badly.

BLACK WOMAN WITH FRIED DRUMSTICK.

Huh. Whiffit.

BEFORE COLUMBUS.

Dragons, of which meanin these dragons they were afeared back then. When they thought thuh worl was flat. They stayed at home. Them thinking thuh worl was flat kept it roun. Them thinkin thuh sun revolved uhroun thuh earth kin kept them satellite-like. They figured out thuh truth and scurried out. Figurin out thuh truth kin put them in their place and they scurried out tuh put us in ours.

YES AND GREENS BLACK-EYED PEAS CORNBREAD.

Mmmmm. Yes. You should write that down. You should write that down and you should hide it under uh rock.

BEFORE COLUMBUS.

Thuh earthsgettin level with thuh land land HO and thuh lands gettin level with thuh sea.

PRUNES AND PRISMS, HAM & OLD MAN RIVER JORDAN.

Not yet—

QUEEN-THEN-PHARAOH HATSHEPSUT.

An I am Sheba she be me. Youll mutter thuh words and part thuh waves and come uhlong come uhlong.

AND BIGGER AND BIGGER AND BIGGER.

I would like tuh be fit in back in thuh storybook from which I camed.

BLACK MAN WITH WATERMELON.

My text was writ in water. I would like tuh drink it down.

QUEEN-THEN-PHARAOH HATSHEPSUT.

Down tuh float drown tuh float down. My son erased his mothers mark.

AND BIGGER AND BIGGER AND BIGGER.

I am grown too big for thuh word thats me.

PRUNES AND PRISMS.

Prunes and prisms prunes and prisms prunes and prisms: 14.

QUEEN-THEN-PHARAOH HATSHEPSUT.

An I am Sheba me am. (She be doo be wah waaaah doo wah.) Come uhlong come on uhlong on.

BEFORE COLUMBUS.

Before Columbus directs thuh traffic: left right left right.

PRUNES AND PRISMS.

Prunes and prisms prunes and prisms.

QUEEN-THEN-PHARAOH HATSHEPSUT.

I left my mark on all I made. My son erase his mothers mark.

BLACK WOMAN WITH FRIED DRUMSTICK.

Where you gonna go now now that you done dieded?

AND BIGGER AND BIGGER AND BIGGER.

Would some body take these straps offuh me please?
Gaw. I would like tuh drink in drown—

BEFORE COLUMBUS.

There is uh tiny land mass just above my reach.

LOTS OF GREASE AND LOTS OF PORK.

There is uh tiny land mass just outside of my vocabulary.

OLD MAN RIVER JORDAN.

Do in dip diddly did-did thuh drop? Drop do it be
dripted? Uh huh.

BEFORE COLUMBUS.

Land:

AND BIGGER AND BIGGER AND BIGGER.

HO!

QUEEN-THEN-PHARAOH HATSHEPSUT.

I saw Columbus comin Before Columbus comin/goin
over tuh meet you—

BEFORE COLUMBUS.

Thuh first time I saw it. It was huge. Thuh green sea
becomes uh hillside. Uh hillside populated with some
peoples I will name. Thuh first time I saw it it was uh
was-huge once one.

Huh. It has been gettin smaller ever since.

QUEEN-THEN-PHARAOH HATSHEPSUT.

Land:

BLACK MAN WITH WATERMELON.

HO!

(A bell sounds once.)

PANEL III: THUH LONESOME 3SOME

BLACK MAN WITH WATERMELON.

It must have rained. Gaw. Must-uh-rained-on-down-on-us-why. Aint that somethin. Must uh rained! Gaw. Our crops have prospered. Must uh rained why aint that somethin why aint that somethin-somethin gaw somethin: nice.

BLACK WOMAN WITH FRIED DRUMSTICK.

Funny.

BLACK MAN WITH WATERMELON.

Gaw. Callin on it spose we did: gaw—thuh uhrainin gaw huh? Gaw gaw. Lookie look-see gaw: where there were riv-lets now there are some. Gaw. Cement tuh mudment accomplished with uh gaw uh flick of my wrist gaw. Huh. Look here now there is uh gaw uh wormlett. Came out tuhday. In my stools gaw gaw gaw gaw they all out tuhday. Come out tuh breathe gaw dontcha? Sure ya dontcha sure gaw ya dontcha sure ya dontcha do yall gaw. Gaw. Our one melon has given intuh 3. Callin what it gived birth callin it gaw. 3 August hams out uh my hands now surroundin me an is all of um mines? GAW. Uh huhn. Gaw Gaw. Cant breathe.

BLACK WOMAN WITH FRIED DRUMSTICK.

Funny how these eggs break when I drop them. Thought they was past that. Huh. 3 broke in uh row. Guess mmm on uh roll uh some sort, huh. Hell. Huh. Whiffit.

BLACK MAN WITH WATERMELON.

Gaw. Gaw. Cant breathe.

BLACK WOMAN WITH FRIED DRUMSTICK.

Some things still hold. Huh. Uh old layed eggull break after droppin most likely. Huh. 4 in uh row. Awe on that.

BLACK MAN WITH WATERMELON.

Gaw. Cant breathe you.

BLACK WOMAN WITH FRIED DRUMSTICK.

You dont need to. No need for breathin for you no more, huh? 5. 6. Mm makin uh history. 7-hhh 8-hhh mm makin uh mess. Huh. Whiffit.

BLACK MAN WITH WATERMELON.

Gaw. Gaw loosen my collar. No air in here.

BLACK WOMAN WITH FRIED DRUMSTICK.

7ssgot uh red dot. Awe on that.

BLACK MAN WITH WATERMELON.

Sweetheart—. SWEETHEART?!

BLACK WOMAN WITH FRIED DRUMSTICK.

9. Chuh. Funny. Funny. Somethin still holdin on. Let me loosen your collar for you you comed home after uh hard days work. Your suit: tied. Days work was runnin from them we know aint chase-ted you. You comed back home after uh hard days work such uh hard days work that now you cant breathe you. Now.

BLACK MAN WITH WATERMELON.

Dont take it off just loosen it. Dont move thuh tree branch let thuh tree branch be.

BLACK WOMAN WITH FRIED DRUMSTICK.

Your days work aint like any others day work: you bring your tree branch home. Let me loosen thuh tie let me loosen thuh neck-lace let me loosen up thuh noose that stringed him up let me leave thuh tree branch be. Let me rub your wrists.

BLACK MAN WITH WATERMELON.

Gaw. Gaw.

BLACK WOMAN WITH FRIED DRUMSTICK.

Some things still hold. Wrung thuh necks of them hens and they still give eggs. Huh: like you. Still sproutin feathers even after they fried. Huh: like you too. 10. Chuh. Eggs still break. Thuh mess makes uh stain. Thuh stain makes uh mark. Whiffit. Whiffit.

BLACK MAN WITH WATERMELON.

They put me on uh platform tuh wait for uh train. Uh who who uh who who uh where ya gonna go now—.

Platform hitched with horses/steeds. Steeds runned off in left me there swinging. It had begun tuh rain. Hands behind my back. This time tied. I had heard of uh word called scaffold and thought that perhaps they just might build me one of um but uh uhn naw just outa my vocabulary but uh uhn naw: trees come cheaply.

BLACK WOMAN WITH FRIED DRUMSTICK.

9. 10. I aint hungry. 10. 11. You dont eat. Dont need to.

BLACK MAN WITH WATERMELON.

Swingin from front tuh back uhgain. Back tuh—back tuh that was how I be wentin. Chin on my chest hangin down in restin eyes each on eyein my 2 feets. Left on thuh right one right one on thuh left. Crossed eyin. It was difficult tuh breathe. Toes uncrossin then crossin for luck. With my eyes. Gaw. It had begun tuh rain. Oh. Gaw. Ever so lightly. Blood came on up. You know: tough. Like riggamartins-stifly only—isolated. They some of em pointed they summoned uh laughed they some looked quick in an then they looked uhway. It had begun tuh rain. I hung on out tuh dry. They puttin uhway their picnic baskets. Ever so lightly gaw gaw it had begun tuh rain. They pullin out their umbrellas in hidedid up, their eyes. Oh.

BLACK WOMAN WITH FRIED DRUMSTICK.

I aint hungry you dont eat 12 13 and thuh floor will shine. Look: there we are. You in me. Reflectin. Hello! Dont move—.

BLACK MAN WITH WATERMELON.

It had begun tuh rain. Now: huh. Sky flew open and thuh light went ZAP. Tree bowed over till thuh branch said BROKE. Uhround my necklace my neck uhround my neck my tree branch. In full bloom. It had begun tuh rain. Feet hit thuh ground in I started runnin. I was wet right through intuh through. I was uh wet that dont get dry. Draggin on my tree branch on back tuh home.

BLACK WOMAN WITH FRIED DRUMSTICK.

On back tuh that.

BLACK MAN WITH WATERMELON.

Gaw. What was that?

BLACK WOMAN WITH FRIED DRUMSTICK.

"On back tuh that"? Huh. Somethin I figured. Huh. Chuh. Lord. Who! Whiffit.

BLACK MAN WITH WATERMELON.

When I dieded they cut me down. Didnt have no need for me no more. They let me go.

BLACK WOMAN WITH FRIED DRUMSTICK.

Thuh lights dimmed in thats what saved you. Lightnin comed down zappin trees from thuh sky. You got uhway!

ALL. (*Except* **BLACK WOMAN.**)

Not exactly.

BLACK WOMAN WITH FRIED DRUMSTICK.

Oh. I see.

BLACK MAN WITH WATERMELON.

They tired of me. Pulled me out of thuh trees then treed me then tired of me. Thats how it has gone. Thats how it be wentin.

BLACK WOMAN WITH FRIED DRUMSTICK.

Oh. I see. Youve been dismissed. But-where-to? Must be somewhere else tuh go aside from just go gone. Huh. Whiffit: huh. You smell.

BLACK MAN WITH WATERMELON.

Im dead. Maybe I should bathe.

BLACK WOMAN WITH FRIED DRUMSTICK.

I call those 3 thuh lonesome 3some. Maybe we should pray.

BLACK MAN WITH WATERMELON.

Thuh lonesome 3some. Spose theyll do.

(*A bell sounds twice.*)

PANEL IV: SECOND CHORUS

OLD MAN RIVER JORDAN.

Come in look tuh look-see.

VOICE ON THUH TEE V.

Good evening this is thuh news. A small sliver of uh tree branch has been found in *The Death of the Last Black Man*. Upon careful examination thuh small sliver of thuh treed branch what was found has been found tuh be uh fossilized bone fragment. With this finding authorities claim they are hot on his tail.

PRUNES AND PRISMS.

Uh small sliver of uh treed branch growed from-tuh uh bone.

AND BIGGER AND BIGGER AND BIGGER.

WILL SOMEBODY WILL THIS ROPE FROM ROUND MY NECK GOD DAMN I WOULD LIKE TUH TAKE MY BREATH BY RIGHTS GAW GAW.

LOTS OF GREASE AND LOTS OF PORK.

This is the death of the last black man in the whole entire world.

(A bell sounds slowly twice.)

BLACK MAN WITH WATERMELON.

I had heard of uh word called scaffold and had hopes they just might maybe build me one but uh uh naw gaw—

HAM.

There was uh tree with your name on it.

BLACK MAN WITH WATERMELON.

Jumpin out of uh tree they chase me tree me back tuh thuh tree. Thats where I be came from. Thats where I be wentin.

YES AND GREENS BLACK-EYED PEAS CORNBREAD.

Someone ought tuh. Write that down.

LOTS OF GREASE AND LOTS OF PORK.

There is a page dogeared at "Histree" hidin just outside my word hoard. Wheres he gonna come to now that he done gone from.

QUEEN-THEN-PHARAOH HATSHEPSUT.

Wheres he gonna go come to now that he gonna go gone on?

OLD MAN RIVER JORDAN.

For that you must ask Ham.

BLACK WOMAN WITH FRIED DRUMSTICK.

Hen?

LOTS OF GREASE AND LOTS OF PORK.

HAM.

QUEEN-THEN-PHARAOH HATSHEPSUT.

Ham.

PRUNES AND PRISMS.

Hmmmm.

(*A bell sounds twice.*)

HAM.

Hams Begotten Tree. (Catchin up to um in medias res that is we takin off from where we stopped up last time.) Huh. NOW: She goned begotten One who in turn begotten Ours. Ours laughed one day uhloud in from thuh sound hittin thuh air smakity sprung up I, you, n He, She, It. They turned in engaged in simple multiplication thus tuh spawn of theirselves one We one You and one called They. (They in certain conversation known as "Them" and in other certain conversation a.k.a. "Us.") Now very simply: Wassername she finally gave intuh It and tugether they broughted forth uh wildish one called simply Yo. Yo gone be wentin much too long without hisself uh comb in from thuh frizzly that resulted comed one called You (polite form). You (polite) birthed herself Mister, Miss, Maam and Sir who in his later years with That brought forth Yuh Fathuh.

Thuh fact that That was uh mother tuh Yuh Fathuh didnt stop them 2 relations from havin relations. Those strange relations between That thuh mother and Yuh Fathuh thuh son brought forth uh odd lot: called: Yes Massuh, Yes Missy, Yes Maam n Yes Suh Mistuh Suh which goes tuh show that relations with your relations produces complications. Thuh children of That and Yuh Fathuh aside from being plain peculiar was all crosseyed. This defect enhanced their multiplicative possibilities, for example. Yes Suh Mistuh Suh breeded with hisself n gived us Wassername, (thuh 2nd) and Wassernickname. (2 twins in birth joinded at thuh lip.) Thuh 2 twins lived next door tuh one called Uhnother bringing forth Themuhns, She, (thuh 2nd) Auntie, Cousin, and Bro who makeshifted continuous compensations for his loud and oderiferous bodily emissions by all thuh time saying excuse me n through his graciousness brought forth They (polite) who had mixed feelins with She (thuh 2nd) thus bringin forth Ussin who then went on tuh have MeMines.

YES AND GREENS BLACK-EYED PEAS CORNBREAD.

Thuh list goes on in on.

HAM.

MeMines gived out 2 offspring one she called Mines after herself thuh uther she called Themuhns named after all them who comed before. Themuhns married outside thuh tribe joinin herself with uh man they called WhoDat Themuhns in WhoDat brought forth only one child called WhoDatDere. Mines joined up with Wasshisname and from that union come AllYall.

ALL.

All us?

HAM.

No. AllYall.

LOTS OF GREASE AND LOTS OF PORK.

This list goes on in on.

HAM.

Ah yes: Yo suddenly if by majic again became productive in after uh lapse of some great time came back intuh circulation to wiggled uhbout with Yes Missy (one of thuh crosseyed daughters of That and Yuh Fathuh). Yo in Yes Missy begottin ThissunRightHere, Us, ThatOne, She (thuh 3rd) and one called Uncle (who from birth was gifted with great singin and dancin capabilities which helped him make his way in life but tended tuh bring shame on his family).

BEFORE COLUMBUS & BLACK MAN WITH WATERMELON.

Shame on his family.

LOTS OF GREASE AND LOTS OF PORK & BLACK MAN WITH WATERMELON.

Shame on his family.

AND BIGGER AND BIGGER AND BIGGER & BLACK MAN WITH WATERMELON.

Shamed on his family gaw.

YES AND GREENS BLACK-EYED PEAS CORNBREAD.

Write *that* down.

OLD MAN RIVER JORDAN.

(Ham seed his daddy Noah neckked. From that seed, comed AllYall.)

(A bell sounds twice.)

AND BIGGER AND BIGGER AND BIGGER.

(Will somebody please will this rope—.)

VOICE ON THUH TEE V.

Good evening. This is thuh news: Whose fault is it?

BLACK MAN WITH WATERMELON.

Saint mines.

VOICE ON THUH TEE V.

Whose fault iszit??!

ALL.

Saint mines!

OLD MAN RIVER JORDAN.

I cant re-member back that far. (Ham can—but uh uh naw gaw—Ham wuduhnt there, huh.)

ALL.

HAM BONE HAM BONE WHERE YOU BEEN ROUN THUH WORL N BACK A-GAIN.

QUEEN-THEN-PHARAOH HATSHEPSUT.

Whatcha seen Hambone girl?

BLACK WOMAN WITH FRIED DRUMSTICK.

Didnt see you. I saw thuh worl.

HAM.

I was there.

PRUNES AND PRISMS.

Didnt see you.

HAM.

I WAS THERE.

VOICE ON THUH TEE V.

Didnt see you.

BLACK MAN WITH WATERMELON & AND BIGGER AND BIGGER AND BIGGER.

THUH BLACK MAN. HE MOOOVE.

ALL.

HAM BONE HAM BONE WHATCHA DO? GOT UH CHANCE N FAIRLY FLEW.

BLACK WOMAN WITH FRIED DRUMSTICK.

Over thuh front yard.

BLACK MAN WITH WATERMELON.

Overshot.

ALL.

6 BY 6 BY 6.

BLACK MAN WITH WATERMELON.

Thats right.

AND BIGGER AND BIGGER AND BIGGER.

WILL SOMEBODY WILL THIS ROPE

ALL.

Good evening. This is the news.

VOICE ON THUH TEE V.

Whose fault is it?

ALL.

Saint mines!

VOICE ON THUH TEE V.

Whose fault iszit?!!

HAM.

SAINT MINES!

(*A bell rings twice.*)

—Ham. Is. Not. Tuh. BLAME! WhoDatDere joinded with one called Sir 9th generation of thuh first Sir son of You (polite) thuh first daughter of You WhoDatDere with thuh 9th Sir begettin forth Him—

BLACK MAN WITH WATERMELON.

Hen?!

ALL. (*Except* **HAM.**)

HIM!

BLACK WOMAN WITH FRIED DRUMSTICK.

Sold.

HAM.

SOLD! allyall[9] not tuh be confused w/allus[12] joined w/ allthem[3] in from that union comed forth wasshisname[21] SOLD wassername[19] still by thuh reputation uh thistree one uh thuh 2 twins loses her sight through fiddlin n falls w/ugly old yuhfathuh[4] given she[8] SOLD whodat[33] pairs w/you[23] (still polite) of which nothinmuch comes nothinmuch now nothinmuch[6] pairs with yessuhmistuhsuh[17] tuh drop one called yo now yo[9-0] still who gone be wentin now w/elle gived us el SOLD let us not forget ye[1-2-5] w/thee[3] givin us thou[9-2] who w/ thuh they who switches their designation in certain conversation yes they[10] broughted forth onemore[2] at thuh same time in thuh same row right next door we

have datone[12] w/disone[14] droppin off duhutherone[2-2]
SOLD let us not forgetyessuhmassuhsuh[38] w/thou[8] who
gived up memines[3-0] SOLD we are now rollin through
thuh long division gimmie uh gimmie uh gimmie uh
squared-off route round it off round it off n round it out
w/sistuh[4-3] who lives with one called saintmines[9] givin
forth one uh year how it got there callin it jessgrew
callin it saintmines callin it whatdat whatdat whatdat
SOLD.

BLACK MAN WITH WATERMELON.

Thuh list goes on and on. Dont it.

ALL.

Ham Bone Ham Bone Ham Bone Ham Bone.

BEFORE COLUMBUS.

Left right left right.

QUEEN-THEN-PHARAOH HATSHEPSUT.

Left left left whose left...?

(A bell sounds twice.)

LOTS OF GREASE AND LOTS OF PORK.

This is the death of the last black man in the whole
entire world.

PANEL V: IN THUH GARDEN OF HOODOO IT

BLACK WOMAN WITH FRIED DRUMSTICK.

Somethins turnin. Huh. Whatizit. —Mercy. Mercy. Huh. Chew on this. Ssuh feather. Sswhatchashud be eatin now ya no. Ssuhfeather: stuffin. Chew on it. Huh. Feathers sprouted from thuh fried hens—dont ask me how. Somethins out uh whack. Somethins out uh rights. Your arms still on your elbows. Im still here. Whensit gonna end. Soon. Huh. Mercy. Thuh Tree. Springtime. And harvest. Huh. Somethins turnin. So many melons. Huh. From one tuh 3 tuh many. Must be nature. Gnaw on this. Gnaw on this, huh? Gnaw on this awe on that.

BLACK MAN WITH WATERMELON.

Aint eatable.

BLACK WOMAN WITH FRIED DRUMSTICK.

I know.

BLACK MAN WITH WATERMELON.

Aint eatable aint it. Nope. Nope.

BLACK WOMAN WITH FRIED DRUMSTICK.

Somethins turnin. Huh. Whatizit.

BLACK MAN WITH WATERMELON.

Aint eatable so I out in out ought not aint be eatin it aint that right. Yep. Nope. Yep. Uh huhn.

BLACK WOMAN WITH FRIED DRUMSTICK.

Huh. Whatizit.

BLACK MAN WITH WATERMELON.

I remember what I like. I remember what my likes tuh eat when I be in thuh eatin mode.

BLACK WOMAN WITH FRIED DRUMSTICK.

Chew on this.

BLACK MAN WITH WATERMELON.

When I be in thuh eatin mode.

BLACK WOMAN WITH FRIED DRUMSTICK.

Swallow it down. I know. Gimme your pit. Needs bathin.

BLACK MAN WITH WATERMELON.

Choice between peas and corns—my feets—. Choice: peas. Choice between peas and greens choice: greens. Choice between greens and potatoes choice: potatoes. Yams. Boiled or mashed choice: mashed. Aaah. Mmm. My likenesses.

BLACK WOMAN WITH FRIED DRUMSTICK.

Mercy. Turns—

BLACK MAN WITH WATERMELON.

My likenesses! My feets! Aaah! SWEET-HEART. Aaah! SPRING-TIME!

BLACK WOMAN WITH FRIED DRUMSTICK.

Spring-time.

BLACK MAN WITH WATERMELON.

SPRING-TIME!

BLACK WOMAN WITH FRIED DRUMSTICK.

Mercy. Turns—

BLACK MAN WITH WATERMELON.

I remembers what I likes. I remembers what I likes tuh eat when I bein in had been in thuh eatin mode. Bein in had been: now in then. I be eatin hen. Hen.

BLACK WOMAN WITH FRIED DRUMSTICK.

Huh?

BLACK MAN WITH WATERMELON.

HEN!

BLACK WOMAN WITH FRIED DRUMSTICK.

Hen?

BLACK MAN WITH WATERMELON.

Hen. Huh. My meals. Aaaah: my meals. *BRACH*-A-LEE.

BLACK WOMAN WITH FRIED DRUMSTICK.

Whatizit. Huh. —GNAW ON THIS! Good. Uhther pit?

BLACK MAN WITH WATERMELON.

We sittin on this porch right now aint we. Uh huhn. Aaah. Yes. Sittin right here right now on it in it ainthuh first time either iduhnt it. Yep. Nope. Once we was here once wuhduhnt we. Yep. Yep. Once we being here. Uh huhn. Huh. There is uh Now and there is uh Then. Ssall there is. (I bein in uh Now: uh Now bein in uh Then: I bein, in Now in Then, in I will be. I was be too but thats uh Then thats past. That me that was-be is uh me-has-been. Thuh Then that was-be is uh has-been-Then too. Thuh me-has-been sits in thuh be-me: we sit on this porch. Same porch. Same me. Thuh Then thats been somehow sits in thuh Then that will be: same Thens. I swing from uh tree. You cut me down and bring me back. Home. Here. I fly over thuh yard. I fly over thuh yard in all over. Them thens stays fixed. Fixed Thens. Thuh Thems stays fixed too. Thuh Thems that come and take me and thuh Thems that greet me and then them Thems that send me back here. Home. Stays fixed, them do.)

BLACK WOMAN WITH FRIED DRUMSTICK.

Your feets.

BLACK MAN WITH WATERMELON.

I: be. You: is. It: be. He, She: thats us (thats it.) We: thats he in she: you aroun me: us be here. You: still is. They: be. Melon. Melon. Melon: mines. I remember all my lookuhlikes. You. You. Remember me.

BLACK WOMAN WITH FRIED DRUMSTICK.

Gnaw on this then swallow it down. Youll have your fill then well put you in your suit coat.

BLACK MAN WITH WATERMELON.

Thuh suit coat I picked out? Thuh stripely one? HA! Peas. Choice: *BRACH*-A-LEE.

BLACK WOMAN WITH FRIED DRUMSTICK.

Chew and swallow please.

BLACK MAN WITH WATERMELON.

Thuh stripely one with thuh fancy patch pockets!

BLACK WOMAN WITH FRIED DRUMSTICK.

Sweetheart.

BLACK MAN WITH WATERMELON.

SPRING-TIME.

BLACK WOMAN WITH FRIED DRUMSTICK.

Sweetheart.

BLACK MAN WITH WATERMELON.

Where am I gonna go now that I done dieded.

BLACK WOMAN WITH FRIED DRUMSTICK.

The time between us will be greater than the time we
had between us. Must be somewhere else tuh go aside
from just go gone.

BLACK MAN WITH WATERMELON.

6 by 6 by 6.

BLACK WOMAN WITH FRIED DRUMSTICK.

Thats right.

BLACK MAN WITH WATERMELON.

Rock reads "HooDoo."

BLACK WOMAN WITH FRIED DRUMSTICK.

Now you know. Know now dontcha. Somethins turnin—.

BLACK MAN WITH WATERMELON.

Who do? Them do. Aint that nice. Huh. Miss me.
Remember me. Missmemissmewhatsmyname.

BLACK WOMAN WITH FRIED DRUMSTICK.

Aaaaah?

BLACK MAN WITH WATERMELON.

Remember me. AAAH.

BLACK WOMAN WITH FRIED DRUMSTICK.

Thats it. Open wide. Here it comes. Stuffin.

BLACK MAN WITH WATERMELON.

Yeeeech.

BLACK WOMAN WITH FRIED DRUMSTICK.

Eat uhnother. Hear. I eat one. You eat one more.

BLACK MAN WITH WATERMELON.

Stuffed. Time tuh go.

BLACK WOMAN WITH FRIED DRUMSTICK.

Not yet!

BLACK MAN WITH WATERMELON.

I got uh way?

BLACK WOMAN WITH FRIED DRUMSTICK.

Huh?

BLACK MAN WITH WATERMELON.

I got uhway?

BLACK WOMAN WITH FRIED DRUMSTICK.

Nope. Yep. Nope. Nope.

BLACK MAN WITH WATERMELON.

Miss me.

BLACK WOMAN WITH FRIED DRUMSTICK.

Miss me.

BLACK MAN WITH WATERMELON.

Re-member me.

BLACK WOMAN WITH FRIED DRUMSTICK.

Re-member me.

BLACK MAN WITH WATERMELON.

My hands are on my wrists. Arms on elbows. Looks: old-fashioned. Nothin fancy there. Toes curl up not down. My feets-now clean. Still got all my teeth. Re-member me.

BLACK WOMAN WITH FRIED DRUMSTICK.

Re-member me.

BLACK MAN WITH WATERMELON.

Call on me sometime.

BLACK WOMAN WITH FRIED DRUMSTICK.

Call on me sometime. Hear? Hear?

(A bell sounds once.)

BLACK WOMAN WITH FRIED DRUMSTICK.

Thuh dirt itself turns itself. So many melons. From one tuh 3 tuh many. Look at um all. Ssuh garden. Awe on that. Winter pro-cessin back tuh back with spring-time. They roll on by us that way. Uh whole line gone roun. Chuh. Thuh worl be roun. Moves that way so they say. You comed back. Yep. Nope. Well. Build uh well.

(A bell sounds twice.)

FINAL CHORUS

BLACK MAN WITH WATERMELON.

"Yes. Oh, me? Chuh, no—"

VOICE ON THUH TEE V.

Good morning. This is thuh news:

BLACK WOMAN WITH FRIED DRUMSTICK.

Somethins turnin. Thuh page.

(A bell sounds twice.)

LOTS OF GREASE AND LOTS OF PORK.

This is the death of the last black man in the whole entire worl.

OLD MAN RIVER JORDAN.

Uh blank page turnin with thuh sound of it. Thuh sound of movin hands.

BLACK WOMAN WITH FRIED DRUMSTICK.

Yesterday today next summer tomorrow just uh moment uhgoh in 1317 dieded thuh last black man in thuh whole entire world. Uh! Oh. Dont be uhlarmed. Do not be afeared. It was painless. Uh painless passin. He falls twenty-three floors to his death.

ALL.

Yes.

BLACK WOMAN WITH FRIED DRUMSTICK.

23 floors from uh passin ship from space tuh splat on thuh pavement.

ALL.

Yes.

BLACK WOMAN WITH FRIED DRUMSTICK.

He have uh head he been keepin under thuh Tee V.

ALL.

Yes.

BLACK WOMAN WITH FRIED DRUMSTICK.

On his bottom pantry shelf.

ALL.

Yes.

BLACK WOMAN WITH FRIED DRUMSTICK.

He have uh head that hurts. Dont fit right. Put it on tuh go tuh thuh store in it pinched him when he walks his thoughts dont got room. He diediduh he did, huh.

ALL.

Yes.

BLACK WOMAN WITH FRIED DRUMSTICK.

Where he gonna go now now now now now that he done diediduh?

ALL.

Yes.

BLACK WOMAN WITH FRIED DRUMSTICK.

Where he gonna go tuh. WASH.

PRUNES AND PRISMS.

Somethins turnin. Thuh page.

AND BIGGER AND BIGGER AND BIGGER.

Somethins burnin. Thuh tongue.

BLACK MAN WITH WATERMELON.

Thuh tongue itself burns.

OLD MAN RIVER JORDAN.

He jumps in thuh river. These words for partin.

YES AND GREENS BLACK-EYED PEAS CORNBREAD.

And you will write them down.

(*A bell sounds three times.*)

BEFORE COLUMBUS.

All these boats passed by my coast.

PRUNES AND PRISMS.

Somethins turnin. Thuh page.

QUEEN-THEN-PHARAOH HATSHEPSUT.

I saw Columbus comin/I saw Columbus comin goin—

QUEEN-THEN-PHARAOH HATSHEPSUT & BEFORE COLUMBUS.

Left left left whose left...?

AND BIGGER AND BIGGER AND BIGGER & BLACK MAN WITH WATERMELON.

Somethins burnin. Thuh page.

BEFORE COLUMBUS.

All those boats passed by me. My coast fell in-to-the-sea. All thuh boats. They stopped for me.

OLD MAN RIVER JORDAN.

Land: HO!

QUEEN-THEN-PHARAOH HATSHEPSUT.

I waved my hands in warnin. You waved back.

BLACK WOMAN WITH FRIED DRUMSTICK.

Somethins burnin. Thuh page.

QUEEN-THEN-PHARAOH HATSHEPSUT.

I have-not seen you since.

ALL.

Oh!

LOTS OF GREASE AND LOTS OF PORK.

This is the death of the last black man in the whole entire worl.

OLD MAN RIVER JORDAN.

Do in diddley dip die-die thuh drop. Do drop be dripted? Why, of course.

AND BIGGER AND BIGGER AND BIGGER.

Somethins burnin. Thuh tongue.

BLACK MAN WITH WATERMELON.

Thuh tongue itself burns itself.

HAM.

...And from that seed comed All Us.

BLACK WOMAN WITH FRIED DRUMSTICK.

Thuh page.

ALL.

6 BY 6 BY 6.

BLACK WOMAN WITH FRIED DRUMSTICK.

Thats right.

(A bell sounds twice.)

ALL.

LAND: HO!

YES AND GREENS BLACK-EYED PEAS CORNBREAD.

You will write it down because if you dont write it down then we will come along and tell the future that we did not exist.

PRUNES AND PRISMS.

You will write it down and you will carve it out of a rock.

(Pause.)

BEFORE COLUMBUS.

You will write down thuh past and you will write down thuh present

VOICE ON THUH TEE V.

and in what in thuh future. You will write it down.

(Pause.)

BIGGER AND BIGGER AND BIGGER.

It will be of us

LOTS OF GREASE AND LOTS OF PORK.

but you will mention them from time to time

YES AND GREENS BLACK-EYED PEAS CORNBREAD.

so that in the future when they come along theyll know how they exist.

(Pause.)

HAM.

It will be for us

OLD MAN RIVER JORDAN.

but you will mention them from time to time

PRUNES AND PRISMS.

so that in the future when they come along theyll know why they exist.

(Pause.)

QUEEN-THEN-PHARAOH HATSHEPSUT.

You will carve it all out of a rock

BIGGER AND BIGGER AND BIGGER.

so that in the future when we come along

YES AND GREENS BLACK-EYED PEAS CORNBREAD.

we will know that the rock does yes exist.

BLACK WOMAN WITH FRIED DRUMSTICK.

Down down down down down down down down—

LOTS OF GREASE AND LOTS OF PORK.

This is the death of the last black man in the whole entire worl.

PRUNES AND PRISMS.

Somethins turnin. Thuh page.

OLD MAN RIVER JORDAN.

Thuh last news of thuh last man:

VOICE ON THUH TEE V.

Good morning. This is thuh last news:

BLACK MAN WITH WATERMELON.

Miss me.

BLACK WOMAN WITH FRIED DRUMSTICK.

Miss me.

BLACK MAN WITH WATERMELON.

Re-member me.

BLACK WOMAN WITH FRIED DRUMSTICK.

Re-member me. Call on me sometime. Call on me sometime. Hear? Hear?

HAM.

In thuh future when they came along we be meeting them. On thuh coast.

ALL.

Uuuuhh!

HAM.

Our coast! We—be—so—po-lite! But. In thuh rock. We wrote: ha ha ha.

ALL.

Ha. Ha. Ha. Ha. Ha. Ha. Ha. Ha. Ha. Ha. Ha. Ha. Ha. Ha. HHHHHHHHHHHHH. HA!

BLACK MAN WITH WATERMELON.

Thuh black man he move. He move. He hans.

BLACK WOMAN WITH FRIED DRUMSTICK.

This is the death of the last black man in the whole entire worl.

(A bell sounds once.)

ALL.

Hold it. Hold it. Hold it. Hold it. Hold it. Hold it. Hold it.

End of Play